For Anna

M.W.

For Sebastian,
David & Candlewick

H.O.

First published 1991 by Walker Books Ltd
87 Vauxhall Walk, London SE11 5HJ

This edition including DVD published 2006

10 9 8 7 6 5

This book has been typeset in Garamond

Printed in China

British Library Cataloguing in Publication Data:
a catalogue record for this book is available
from the British Library

ISBN-13: 978-1-4063-0364-3
ISBN-10: 1-4063-0364-X

www.walkerbooks.co.uk

FARMER DUCK

written by
MARTIN WADDELL

illustrated by
HELEN OXENBURY

WALKER BOOKS
AND SUBSIDIARIES
LONDON • BOSTON • SYDNEY • AUCKLAND

There once was a duck
who had the bad luck to live
with a lazy old farmer.
The duck did the work.
The farmer stayed
all day in bed.

The duck fetched the cow from the field.

"How goes the work?" called the farmer.

The duck answered,

"Quack!"

The duck brought the sheep from the hill.

"How goes the work?" called the farmer.

The duck answered,

"Quack!"

The duck put the hens in their house.

"How goes the work?"

called the farmer.

The duck answered,

"Quack!"

The farmer got fat through staying in bed
and the poor duck got fed up
with working all day.

"How goes the work?"

"Quack!"

"How goes the work?"

"Quack!"

"How goes the work?"

"Quack!"

"How goes the work?"

"Quack!"

"How goes the work?"

"Quack!"

"How goes the work?"

"Quack!"

The poor duck was sleepy

and weepy

and tired.

The hens and the cow and the sheep got very upset.
They loved the duck.
So they held a meeting under the moon and they made a plan for the morning.

"Moo!"
said the cow.

"Baa!"
said the sheep.

"Cluck!"
said the hens.

And *that* was the plan!

It was just before dawn and the farmyard was still.
Through the back door and into the house
crept the cow and the sheep
and the hens.

They stole
down the hall.
They creaked
up the stairs.

They squeezed under the bed of
the farmer and wriggled about.
The bed started to rock
and the farmer woke up,
and he called,
"How goes the work?"
and…

"M o o!"

"B a a!"

"C l u c k!"

They lifted his bed
and he started to shout,
and they banged and they bounced
the old farmer about and about and about,
right out of the bed…

and he fled with the cow and the sheep and the hens

mooing and baaing and clucking around him.

Down the lane...

"Moo!"

through the fields...

"Baa!"

over the hill…

“Cluck!”

and he never came back.

The duck awoke and
waddled wearily into the
yard expecting to hear,
"How goes the work?"
But nobody spoke!

Then the cow and the sheep
and the hens came back.

"Quack?" asked the duck.

"Moo!" said the cow.

"Baa!" said the sheep.

"Cluck!" said the hens.

Which told the duck
the whole
story.

Then mooing and baaing
and clucking and quacking
they all set to work
on their farm.